A NOTE TO PARENTS

When your children are ready to "step into reading," giving them the right books—and lots of them—is as crucial as giving them the right food to eat. **Step into Reading Books** present exciting stories and information reinforced with lively, colorful illustrations that make learning to read fun, satisfying, and worthwhile. They are priced so that acquiring an entire library of them is affordable. And they are beginning readers with an important difference—they're written on four levels.

    Step 1 Books, with their very large type and extremely simple vocabulary, have been created for the very youngest readers. **Step 2 Books** are both longer and slightly more difficult. **Step 3 Books,** written to mid-second-grade reading levels, are for the child who has acquired even greater reading skills. **Step 4 Books** offer exciting nonfiction for the increasingly proficient reader.

    Children develop at different ages. **Step into Reading Books,** with their four levels of reading, are designed to help children become good—and interested—readers *faster*. The grade levels assigned to the four steps—preschool through grade 1 for Step 1, grades 1 through 3 for Step 2, grades 2 and 3 for Step 3, and grades 2 through 4 for Step 4—are intended only as guides. Some children move through all four steps very rapidly; others climb the steps over a period of several years. These books will help your child "step into reading" in style!

Text copyright © 1990 by Random House, Inc. Illustrations copyright © 1990 by Normand Chartier. All rights reserved under International and Pan-American Copyright Conventions. Published in the United States by Random House, Inc., New York, and simultaneously in Canada by Random House of Canada Limited, Toronto.

Library of Congress Cataloging-in-Publication Data:
Hayward, Linda. All stuck up / by Linda Hayward ; illustrated by Normand Chartier. p. cm. — (Step into reading. A Step 1 book) SUMMARY: Brer Fox makes a tar baby in order to catch Brer Rabbit. ISBN: 0-679-80216-9 (pbk.); 0-679-90216-3 (lib. bdg.) [1. Folklore, Afro-American. 2. Animals— Folklore.] I. Chartier, Normand, ill. II. Title. III. Series: Step into reading. A Step 1 book. PZ8. 1.H3245A1 1990 398.2'452'08996073—dc20 [E] 89-34675

Manufactured in the United States of America 9 0

STEP INTO READING is a trademark of Random House, Inc.

Step into Reading

All Stuck Up

By Linda Hayward
Illustrated by Normand Chartier

A Step 1 Book

Random House New York

Brer Fox is
always thinking
of ways to catch
Brer Rabbit.

Brer Rabbit is
always thinking
of ways to not
get caught!

Today Brer Fox mixes up
some mighty sticky stuff.
This time he is sure
Brer Rabbit won't get away!

He fixes up something
that looks like a boy.

He puts it down
on the road
by the brier patch.

Then he jumps
into the bushes
and waits.

By and by
Brer Rabbit
comes along.

"Howdy, Mr. Boy!"
he calls.
"Nice day, isn't it?"
Mr. Boy doesn't answer.

"Can't you hear?"

yells Brer Rabbit.

"I said HOWDY!"

Mr. Boy doesn't answer.
"Talk or I'll bop you,"
says Brer Rabbit.
Still no word
from Mr. Boy.

Brer Rabbit lets
him have it.
He bops him
with both fists.

He kicks him
with both feet.

Pretty soon
Brer Rabbit is
all stuck up.

Out comes Brer Fox!

Brer Rabbit is

stew meat, for sure.

"I am going to throw you
in a pot and boil you,"
says Brer Fox.
"I don't care,"
says Brer Rabbit.
"Just don't throw me
in that brier patch!"
Brer Fox is surprised.
Maybe it's too hot to cook!

"Guess I'll have to hang you," says Brer Fox. "That's fine with me," says Brer Rabbit. "Just don't throw me in that brier patch!"

Brer Fox thinks again.
Maybe hanging
is a bad idea!

"Then I'll drown you,"
says Brer Fox.

"Boil me, hang me, drown me, skin me, but please, *PLEASE* don't throw me in that brier patch!" cries Brer Rabbit.

"I know!" says Brer Fox.
"I'll throw you in
   that brier patch!"

Brer Fox pulls
Brer Rabbit free.

Then he takes him
and throws him
right into the middle
of the brier patch.

Brer Fox begins
to dance around.
Whoo-eee!
Brer Rabbit is
gone for good.

But wait!
What's that
on the other side
of the brier patch?

It's Brer Rabbit!

"Yoo-hoo, Brer Fox,"
he calls.

"Guess who loves
the brier patch?
Me!
This is the place
where I was born!"

Brer Fox isn't
dancing anymore.
That Brer Rabbit
has tricked him again.
But just wait!
Next time he will
get him, for sure.